This book belongs to...

_____

© Illus. Dr. Seuss 1957

Adapted from "Uncle Willy and the Pirates" in _Richard Scarry's Funniest Storybook Ever_
© 1972 by Richard Scarry.
Text and illustrations © 1994 by Richard Scarry. All rights reserved under International and
Pan-American Copyright Conventions. Published in the United States by Random House, Inc.,
New York, and simultaneously in Canada by Random House of Canada Limited, Toronto.

Grolier Books is a division of Grolier Enterprises, Inc.

Library of Congress Cataloging-in-Publication Data:
Scarry, Richard. [Pie Rats ahoy!] Richard Scarry's Pie rats ahoy! p. cm. — (Step into reading.
Step 1 book) SUMMARY: Uncle Willy uses a clever disguise to save his boat from a gang of pirates and
make Busytown Bay safe again. ISBN 0-679-84760-X (pbk.) — 0-679-94760-4 (lib. bdg.) [1. Pirates—
Fiction. 2. Animals—Fiction.] I. Title. II. Series. PZ7.S327Rlj 1994 [E]—dc20 92-50998.

Manufactured in the United States of America

Random House, Inc. New York, Toronto, London, Sydney, Auckland

GROLIER
B O O K S
BOOK CLUB EDITION

Richard Scarry's
PIE RATS
AHOY!

BEGINNER BOOKS

A Division of Random House, Inc.

Random House 🏠 New York

BEWARE

There were pirates
on the prowl
in the Busytown Bay.
No one was safe.

But that didn't stop
Uncle Willy.

He was going sailing—
pirates or no pirates.

Off he sailed with a
cherry pie for lunch—

under the bridge,

past the rocks
and around the point—

until he came
to a small island.

Splash!
Uncle Willy dropped
the anchor.

"I think I'll take
a little nap
before I eat
my pie," he said.

He curled up
and went to sleep.
Z-z-z-z-z-z-z.

Ahoy, there,
Uncle Willy!
Pirates are
coming aboard!

"Look out,
you landlubber!"
cried the Pirate King.
"Prepare to meet
your doom."

The pirates gave
Uncle Willy
the old heave-ho.

Then they made
short work of
Uncle Willy's pie.
"Yo ho ho,"
sang the pirates.

"Oh no no,"
Uncle Willy
cried.

He was stuck on an island
with nothing but grass
and shells and driftwood
and a spiky palm tree.

Suddenly he had an idea.

He made some cloth
out of the grass.

He made a head out of
the driftwood.

He made eyes and teeth
out of the shells.

He made a tail out of
a spiky palm leaf.

Then
Uncle Willy
got inside.
Yo ho ho!
A monster crocodile!

Look out,
you pirates!
Prepare to meet
your doom!

Uncle Willy swam out
to the boat.

"Shiver me timbers!"
cried the Pirate King.
"It's a croc!"

The pirates all ran
into the cabin
to hide.

Uncle Willy Crocodile
went aboard and
locked the door.

Then he sailed back
to the dock.

When the people
saw the monster
crocodile coming,
they ran for their lives.

But it was only
Uncle Willy.

Officer Murphy led
those greedy
pie rats away.

Hooray for Uncle Willy!
He has made it safe
to sail again in
Busytown Bay.

I CAN READ IT ALL BY MYSELF

Beginner Books